The Secret of the Fourth Candle

(formerly The Four Candles)

Patricia M. St. John

Scripture Union
47 Marylebone Lane, London W1M 6AX

Other books by Patricia St John:
Treasures of the Snow
Rainbow Garden
Star of Light
The Tanglewoods' Secret

The Secret of the Fourth Candle was first published in
English as The Four Candles with The Cloak 1956
Reprinted 1956
Reprinted with The Guest 1974
Reprinted as The Secret of the Fourth Candle 1978

ISBN 0 85421 586 7

Photoset in Malta by St Paul's Press Limited
Printed in Great Britain by William Clowes & Sons Limited
London, Beccles and Colchester

Contents

The Four Candles

The First Candle

It was still early morning and Aisha stood in the doorway of her home watching the bright winter day break over the sea. The air was cold but very, very clear – so clear that she could even see the Rock of Gibraltar couched like an old lion at the headland. The rising sun threw a silver path of light, so that it looked to Aisha as though she could run across to it and spring on its back. Then her gaze wandered homewards, past the white sails of the fishing boats and the sparkling waters of the harbour, past the tall buildings round the bay, and came to rest on the house in the middle of the town where her mother went to work four days a week.

She had heard so much about that house that it was difficult to believe she had never been inside it, and still more difficult to believe that she had never met the fair-haired child with the strange foreign name who lived there. Aisha knew so much about her; she knew just what time she got up in the morning, what she had for breakfast and the colours of the many little dresses she wore. She knew that this entrancing little girl went to school with her nurse every day and came back about the hour of the afternoon prayer call, and played in a room full of sunshine and books and toys. Her mother, who cleaned the nursery on the nursery-maid's day off, told her about it nearly every day and Aisha never, never got tired of hearing.

So when Aisha wasn't kneading the bread, or sweeping the house, or fetching water from the well, or chasing the goat, or grinding the flour, or washing the clothes, or pulling the babies out of mischief, she liked to stand in the doorway and gaze at the white house far off in the city and dream about the little girl. But just at this time of the year she could not see it very clearly, because the mimosa tree at the bottom of the garden was in flower, and partly hid it. Yet, through the golden sunkissed quivering mass of blossoms, she could still just see the white walls.

'Aisha,' called her mother's voice quite calmly, as though she was saying something perfectly ordinary, 'you had better come and help me today, and Safea must look after the little ones as best she can. It is Sunday, and on Sunday they have visitors and there is much cleaning and so many plates to wash up that I just can't manage alone; although why they can't all eat out of one dish like we do, instead of having three plates each and making all that work, I don't know!'

Aisha turned quickly, her cheeks bright pink, her eyes sparkling, and her heart as golden and dancing as the mimosa tree. For months past she had begged her mother to let her go with her just once, and her mother had always said, 'No, you must stay and look after the other children.' Now her dream was coming true all by itself and she hadn't even asked! Too happy to speak, she ran to the bucket and scrubbed her face and hands till they shone, smoothed down her thick black hair and put a clean towel over her head. She wished she had a clean cotton gown to match, but there wasn't one.

Now she was ready, dancing first on one foot and then on the other, while her mother gave final instructions to poor little Safea who was only seven years old and small for her age. '... and don't let the baby fall into the well,' said her mother, 'and don't let the goat get through the fence and don't let the cat drink the milk.'

'Come on, mother, we shall be late,' shouted Aisha, and danced off down the hill, brushing the sweeping boughs of the mimosa tree and covering her nose with pollen. She did not wish her baby to fall into the well, but the goat and the cat could do what they liked. Nothing mattered today; she was going to fairyland. Her mother caught her up and boxed her ears for behaving in such a wild unruly fashion, and she nine years old! She didn't really mind, because her mother boxed her ears most days, but never very hard. She merely dodged out of reach and skipped happily on, across the common where the donkeys grazed and the wild broom flamed in summer, on to the white road that wound between eucalyptus trees; through a dip in the hills the sea sparkled blue and silver, and the exciting noises of the town began to grow nearer.

They pushed their way through the native quarter and reached the broad Boulevard with its big shops all shut because it was Sunday. The white house where the little girl lived was at the far end of the Boulevard up a flight of marble steps. Aisha suddenly felt rather frightened and walked sedately.

Her mother knocked at the front door, which was opened by another servant, and Aisha with a beating heart stepped over the threshold of her palace of dreams. It was a little bit disappointing; just a rather dark hall with a staircase leading upwards; she only had time to glance at it, before she was bustled into the kitchen and told, without further ceremony, to scrub the floor.

But she was not really disappointed, because, although the kitchen floor was very large to scrub, and Fatima the cook very cross, and her breakfast of the scantiest because she wasn't really supposed to be there, she had seen the staircase; and at the top of the staircase lived the child with the golden hair and one day Aisha would tiptoe up very softly and see her, and they would smile shyly at each other, because, after all, they were both little girls. She forgot all about her aching back and gazed rapturously into the scrubbing bucket until recalled by

4

Fatima who yelled at her not to dawdle.

The winter day sped by; Aisha wiped the dishes and trembled at the terrible judgments which Fatima vowed would fall on her if she broke one. Then she scoured the pans and cleaned the dustbins and scrubbed the scullery, and by that time dusk was falling; the street lamps burned on the Boulevards and the lights from the ships zigzagged in the purple waters of the harbour. Aisha, standing alone in the kitchen, her work finished, stretched her tired body and stood listening. Her mother was cleaning some back yard and Fatima was comfortably asleep by the fire. She was quite alone; she tiptoed to the kitchen door, out into the passage, and stood, with her hands tightly clasped and her face lifted, at the bottom of the staircase.

It was a long staircase, but at the top of it there was a door half open and a light shone out into the passage. It was a soft friendly welcoming light, and Aisha suddenly forgot to be afraid. She scuttled up the staircase toward it on silent bare feet, and peeped into the room.

A little golden-haired girl was standing by a table. And on the table was a wreath of twined evergreens with four white candles. Three of the candles had not been lit, but the fourth burned with a pure light, reflected in the starry eyes of the little girl.

It was the prettiest sight Aisha had ever seen in her life. For one moment she stood breathless, gazing, and then her mother's voice in the kitchen recalled her. She scuttled down the staircase as swiftly and noiselessly as she had scuttled up it and stood meekly waiting in the passage.

And her mother never knew that she had been to fairyland! She thought she had been standing in the passage all the time, and together they left the house and made their way up the lighted Boulevard, her mother grumbling at the lateness of the hour, the little girl seeing one pure white candle burning alone in every street lamp, and the starry eyes of the child reflecting the light.

The Second Candle

The week passed very quickly and Aisha washed and scrubbed and hauled the baby out of mischief as usual; but somehow it was quite different from all the other weeks. The one white candle burning in its wreath of evergreen shed its radiance over all her waking hours and even flickered in her dreams.

The question was, would she be allowed to go again? Sunday at home under the rule of Safea had not been entirely successful. The goat had eaten Monday's dinner and the baby had fallen over the cat and got itself scratched on the nose; not that it was really Safea's fault; it was the sort of accident that might have happened to anyone, but the baby's red nose kept reminding its mother that Safea was not really fit to be left in charge. On Friday Aisha put a little flour on the scar and hoped her mother would forget about it.

She didn't forget. In fact, she grumbled a great deal and all Saturday Aisha's fate hung in the balance. But on Sunday morning it was raining, and rain meant dirty floors and the passages to scrub several times a day. Aisha's mother had a headache and decided to risk the baby.

'Come along, Aisha,' she said crossly as she draped herself in her big white cotton wrap that covered her from top to toe. 'You'll have to help me again today whether you like it or not, and Safea, if you don't look after the baby I'll give you such a thrashing!'

Safea nodded calmly and went on munching her breakfast. Her mother's bark was much worse than her bite and the many thrashings she promised her children very seldom happened. If she did actually pick up a stick, one had only to dodge into the garden and go for a little run. In five minutes mother would have forgotten all about it and would be laughing and throwing the baby in the air.

'Yes, mother, I'll come and help you,' replied Aisha dutifully, and together they splashed their way down the slippery hillside and across the muddy common. Into the town, and up the marble steps and in at the front door they went, and once again Aisha scrubbed the great big kitchen and dried the crockery with bated breath and listened to Fatima's terrible threats of what would happen if she broke anything. In fact the day passed exactly as the Sunday before, until just half an hour before it was time to go home. And then Aisha's adventures began.

The tea-tray with its delicately fluted china cups had been carried down from the drawing room; cross Fatima stood at the sink washing them and handing them to Aisha to dry. Her mother had disappeared into the back yard and dusk was falling. The child was very tired, and her weary thoughts kept straying up the staircase to the room with the lighted candle. In her daydream the flame flickered a little, lapping her with warmth and comfort. She had nearly fallen asleep.

Crash! The fluted cup had slipped from her hand and splintered into a hundred fragments on the stone floor.

Aisha started stupidly for a second and was then recalled by a hard blow on the head. Cross Fatima was screaming with rage and her strong red hand was raised to strike the little girl again.

'You wicked little wretch,' she yelled, 'and the mistress doesn't so much as know you are in the house. Your mother shall take the blame for this, not me.'

Her hand came down hard, but Aisha dodged it and fled as swiftly as a little bird from the kitchen. She was almost blind with panic and fear and there was only one place in this great, cold, unfriendly house where she could be safe. She would take refuge where that little white flame burned in the darkness. Surely no anger or terror could follow her there.

She disappeared into the passage, and Fatima, striking her hand on the table instead of on Aisha, was too hurt to run after her for a moment or two. Then she waddled out in pursuit, but the front door being open she supposed the child had fled into the street, and went back to the kitchen snarling with rage.

Aisha made straight for the staircase. She glanced up just once and saw the light of the open door, blurred through her tears, welcoming her. She sprang up the stairs like a frightened rabbit to its burrow, rushed into the nursery, slammed the door behind her and flung herself, sobbing and trembling, on to the floor at the feet of the little girl.

The little girl, whose name was Petra, stared at her in astonishment and concern. She was a kind little girl and it troubled her to see a child no older than herself in such trouble. She longed to ask her what was the matter but unfortunately they couldn't speak the same language.

It might, however, comfort her to see the lovely thing that Petra had just been doing, so she poked Aisha on the shoulder until she looked up, and having once looked up she stopped in the middle of a loud wail, took a deep breath, and stared and stared at the scene in front of her.

There was the table and the wreath of twined

evergreens with four white candles. Two had not been lit but two burned with a clear white light, reflected in the happy eyes of Petra and in the tears of Aisha.

Two candles this week – and last week there had only been one! And Petra was smiling and pointing to them as though they had some happy secret to tell – some secret of peace and gentleness and stillness, far, far removed from cross Fatima and the cold unfriendly kitchen. Her heart felt all warm and unafraid and she smiled back and drew closer to the little girl, till her dirty ragged skirt brushed the exquisite white folds of Petra's Sunday dress; but neither of them noticed.

Suddenly lots and lots of questions surged up in Aisha's mind and she longed so much to be able to ask them, and yet couldn't, that the tears welled up in her eyes again. Why did they light one the week before and two this week, and when would they light the third and the fourth, and what would happen when they were all alight? She pointed to the candles not yet lit and motioned to Petra to light them.

But Petra shook her curls very emphatically. Apparently such a thing was not to be thought of. She looked quite shocked at such an idea.

But as they stood quietly by the table, the little princess of plenty and the ragged servant child, one in spirit, and happy together, a step was heard coming down the passage, a horrid outside sound, shattering the bright wall of peace and safety that the candle-light seemed to have thrown round Aisha. She suddenly re-membered with a start that she was not safe at all; she was a bold little trespasser who had pushed her way into a place where she had no right to be. Her eyes grew wide with terror and she bolted for the door and began to run down the dark staircase as noiselessly as she had come up it.

But Petra was as quick as she was. She was a very lonely little girl shut away in her grand nursery with no brothers or sisters, and the sud-den appearance of a bright-eyed tousle-haired stranger who crept out of the dark into the magic circle of her candle-light and who seemed to understand what a wonderful occasion was the lighting of the second candle, was as good as an adventure in a story book. She must not let her disappear for ever like that. There was one language of which they both probably under-stood a few words, and that was Spanish, for Petra had picked up a little at school; she darted to the top of the staircase and called softly after the flying figure.

'Venga – Domingo otro.'
(Come again – next Sunday.)

Then she darted back just in time, and was standing demurely if a little breathlessly by the table when Zohra, the nursery maid, a kindly woman who spoke a little of Petra's language, came in with a bucket of coals to make up the fire.

But Zohra as she came along the passage had

not noticed the flying shadow on the staircase, nor did she guess Petra's secret. And Aisha's mother, trundling down the Boulevard bewailing the breakage of that cup, knew nothing about the secret either. It was locked up tight in the hearts of two little girls.

Aisha knew quite a lot of Spanish. She had learned it from the gypsy children who lived in the bamboo enclosure just below theirs, and she had heard the message and understood perfectly.

And that week the rustling of the mimosa tree breathed out three words to her – three words whispered urgently and softly from a height above her, from the white sanctuary of the light of two candles –

'Come again – next Sunday.'

The Third Candle

Sunday was drawing to a close and the Boulevard was a blaze of light and festivity. Only one more Sunday before Christmas, and the great shop windows were wonderfully gay. And at sunset that evening Petra and her mother had lit the third Advent candle.

'And,' said Petra, 'when I light the fourth it will be time to hang up my stocking!'

Her mother laughed and kissed her and told her to run along because on Sunday night Petra's mother usually went to a party and she was in a hurry to be off. Petra nestled longingly against her and clung to her for a moment. She loved the feel of her mother's cool satin dress, the softness of her fur cape and the sweet smell of her cheeks. If only her mother was not quite so pretty and admired she would not have to go to quite so many parties! Then she would have time to come up to the nursery and stand in the beautiful white circle of the three Christmas candles and whisper lovely Christmas secrets. Now the car was at the door and mother was off and away down the passage with a delicious rustle of flouncy skirts. Petra gave a little sigh and climbed the staircase alone, her evergreen wreath in her hand.

But she did not really mind about her mother tonight, because tonight undoubtedly the funny little girl would come, and Zohra would talk to her in her own language and tell her all about the candles, and she would show her the Christmas presents all wrapped up in holly-paper put away in a private drawer. She laid her precious light on the table and went in search of Zohra and the coal bucket.

'Zohra,' said Petra in her most wheedling tones, 'I want you to stay with me tonight. I have a secret and you must help me.'

Zohra had no idea what a secret was, but she was always ready to help her adored Petra, so she smiled indulgently, laid down her bucket of coals, and sat down by the fire to wait and see what might be required of her. One never knew with Petra. She sometimes did have the strangest ideas.

'There is a little girl coming to see me,' explained Petra importantly, 'and she only speaks your language. I want you to tell her what I tell you and I want to show her my Christmas presents.'

This sounded innocent enough. Zohra smiled enthusiastically and nodded; probably, she thought, this was a little school friend, the daughter of some rich Moor, whose mother was bringing her to call.

But just at that moment there was a tiny rustle and movement, and the smile died on Zohra's countenance and gave place to a look of extreme indignation. For round the door there appeared a tousled head wrapped up in an extremely dirty cloth, and a pair of bright anxious eyes set in a smutty little face. The bright eyes did not see Zohra at first. They gazed enraptured at the three candles burning on the table, and the lips parted.

'There she is!' cried Petra joyfully, and she rushed to the door, dragged her disreputable companion into the room, and slammed it behind her. 'I *knew* you'd come,' she said to Aisha. 'Look, I've lit the third candle!'

Aisha could not understand a word but she was delighted at the warmth of the child's welcome, and for a moment her face glowed with love and joy. Then it suddenly turned blank with fear for she had caught sight of Zohra in the shadows and Zohra's face was anything but welcoming. Aisha turned and made a dash for the door but Petra stood in the way and grabbed hold of her firmly.

'You are not to run away!' she said imperiously. 'I am going to tell you all about my candles. Zohra, you are to tell everything I say to this little girl, so she can understand it, in Arabic.'

Zohra shook her head helplessly. She recognized Aisha – the grimy child who scrubbed the scullery on Sundays. How the impertinent little creature had ever got into the nursery was more than she could understand, and she was quite sure Petra's mother would be very angry.

'Your mother wouldn't like it,' said Zohra in her broken speech. 'You know she wouldn't.'

'My mother's gone to a party,' retorted Petra impatiently. 'Don't be silly, Zohra. Do what I tell you. This little girl is my friend. Tell her that I light one candle every week on Sunday night for the coming of the Baby Jesus. Tell her that next week is the feast of His coming. Tell her to be sure to come back next week and see, because on Sunday I shall light all four candles and hang up my stocking and then it will be Christmas.'

Zohra sighed, but decided that the best way to get rid of this unwelcome little visitor was to do what Petra wanted. So she repeated the first two sentences in Arabic like a parrot, but allowed herself a little poetic licence with the rest. 'She says,' explained Zohra, 'that she lights one candle every week for the coming of the Baby Jesus and next week is the feast of His coming and she will light them all – but what you think you are doing here I don't know, you naughty little thing, and don't let me ever catch you in this nursery again or I'll hand you straight over to Fatima in the kitchen.'

Aisha gazed at her sorrowfully and doubtfully. The three candles were burning just as she had known they would be burning, but somehow it was all spoiled. The white circle of light was no longer a welcoming sanctuary of purity and gentleness; there was someone who didn't want her and she felt afraid and wanted to run away.

But perhaps it didn't matter, because the little girl most certainly did want her and the little girl was, after all, queen of the nursery. Now she suddenly took Aisha's hand and drew her to a corner of the nursery and opened a drawer full of parcels done up in holly-paper and golden string.

'Tell her they are my presents, Zohra,' commanded Petra, 'presents for everyone in the house and all my uncles and aunts. And tell her that if she'll come again next Sunday I will make a present for her.'

'She says they are her presents,' interpreted Zohra, 'and now for mercy's sake do get back to the kitchen and don't come up here again, there's a good child!'

She did not speak unkindly, for Aisha was a child of her own race, and probably meant no harm, but she was frightened of being scolded if such a very sooty greasy creature were found in Petra's nursery. If only she could get rid of her now, she would speak to Fatima about it before next Sunday. Fatima would certainly prevent such a thing ever happening again.

Aisha looked awestruck at the candles, and then back at the presents, and almost forgot Zohra. She knew at last why the little girl lit one more candle every week. It was in honour of a Baby called Jesus who was coming next week, and then all the candles would burn and the whole room would be white and radiant and the Baby would laugh and crow. She had never heard of Jesus before, for she was a Moslem girl, but she felt sure He must be a very important Baby to have the candles lit specially for His coming. And all those presents, too! She supposed they were all for Him and she wondered what was inside them − lovely little garments perhaps, and toys and tiny coloured shoes. She wanted to see Him more than she had ever wanted to see anything else in the world. If only that woman would stop looking at her so disapprovingly and spoiling it all. She suddenly became conscious of Zohra again, and shyness and fear overcame her. She gave one quick grateful smile at the little girl, bolted for the door and made off down the stairs as swiftly and silently as she had come. But before she reached the bottom again the clear urgent voice of Petra called after her.

'Venga – Domingo otro.'

Aisha's mother was in a hurry to get back home that night but she had hard work in getting her daughter up the Boulevard. Aisha seemed lost in a dream, dawdling, pressing her nose against every shop window until her mother slapped her.

She did not mind much. There were such lovely things in the shops and although she hadn't a single peseta of her own she wanted them all for the Baby. That tiny pink rabbit-wool coat for instance, He would look sweet in that; and that bright stick of sugar-candy – surely He would enjoy that! Already she loved Him passionately with all the love of her newly-awakened little heart, and one great idea was slowly possessing her. She would give Him a present, too. Next Sunday she would steal up-stairs into the room where the four candles would be burning. She would not stay – just see Him for an instant, kiss His chubby hand and lay her present at His darling feet with the curly baby toes, and then slip back into the dark, satisfied.

The question was, what present could she take Him?

The Gift

She thought of little else all that week. It rained nearly every day, the cold, torrential winter rain of North Africa, and the children crouched round a clay pot of burning charcoal and tried to warm their stiff fingers and toes. The goats and hens came into the house for shelter and were very much in the way and underfoot. The roof leaked, the baby coughed and wailed and snuffled, and everybody got on everybody else's nerves. It was a most trying week for everyone—except for Aisha, who nearly drove her mother crazy by her dreamy absent-mindedness and the stupid new habit she had acquired of sitting gazing into the charcoal, apparently quite unconscious of all the turmoil around her.

She saw wonderful pictures in the charcoal; pictures of herself kneeling, glorified by the candle-light, her hands piled with glittering gifts at the feet of a Baby Who crowed and stretched out His arms towards her and Who seemed in some mysterious way to radiate love and joy. Sometimes, when she was asleep at night cuddled under a sheepskin with Safea, the Baby came right into her arms and she felt, in her dreams, the warmth of His sturdy little body pressed against her and knew that if she could only hold Him fast she would never be lonely or afraid again. Then she would wake to the coldness of the grey morning, with the drip of the rain through the thatch, and to the bitter realization of empty arms and empty hands – for after all, what could she take Him?

Nothing – she had nothing at all! Gradually the truth forced itself upon her and she stood depressed in the doorway gazing at the spoiled mimosa tree, when her mother seized her by the shoulder and gave her a good shake. 'You do nothing all day but stand and stare,' shouted her outraged mother. 'You are no more use in the house than a cow – and the baby has spilled the grain under your very nose! Now go to the well and bring me two buckets of water quickly and don't stand all the afternoon staring into the water.'

She gave her a final push through the doorway and out into the grey rain. Aisha sighed and picked up her bucket and set off shivering. It was horrible going to the well this weather, but there was no help for it. She ran as fast as she could, clatter, clatter down the hill, but she couldn't run back. The hill was very steep and the buckets very heavy and the merciless rain half-blinded her; and worst of all she had no present for the Baby. She was miserable!

Walking with her head well down she bumped straight into old black Msouda who was also going to the well, grumbling, mumbling, moaning and shivering. Black Msouda lived in the hut next to Aisha and it was very hard on her having to draw water at her age, but the orphan grandson who lived with her had broken his arm and there was no one else to do it. She was very angry with Aisha for pushing into her and Aisha was just about to be rude back when she noticed that the old woman was crying: hopeless little sobs of weariness and cold and weakness came from under the towel that covered her bowed head.

Silver candle-light and a smiling Babe who radiated warmth and gentleness and love – an old woman slipping in the mud, weeping with weariness and cold. Aisha suddenly felt terribly sorry for her. She set her buckets down in a safe place by the side of the path and took Msouda's buckets out of her hands.

'I'll fetch your water, Msouda,' she said. 'You go back home.' She turned back down the path leaving the old woman gaping with astonishment. When she returned, Msouda had gone into her hut and was busy looking for something under the trestle that served for a bed.

Aisha set down the buckets in the doorway with a clatter and turned to go, but Msouda suddenly came out from under the bed and ran after her and thrust something soft and sticky into her hand.

'You are a good girl,' she said, 'and I'll give you one of my newly baked khaif.'

Aisha stood quite still in the rain, staring at her treasure, her heart suddenly flooded with joy and sunshine, because there is nothing babies like better than khaif. It is a sort of flat flaky concoction of flour and water, sprinkled in oil and baked on a flat pan. Babies eat it in greasy little pawfuls, and get very oily and happy in the process.

She was so excited that she ran home as far as the bamboo fence without her buckets, and then suddenly remembered and had to go back for them. Fortunately her mother had not seen her. She walked back into the house as though nothing had happened, and nobody knew about the wonderful secret she was hugging inside her.

She had no pretty paper like Petra but she chose a couple of flat shiny leaves and hid her khaif between them and placed it in a safe corner under the sheepskin. At night she took it to bed with her. It does not matter if you lie on top of a khaif because it is flat in any case.

Conveying it to town next day without her mother seeing was difficult, as Aisha's clothes were of the scantiest. She laid it on top of her head and put the towel over it and walked with extreme caution and dignity. By the time she reached the big house she had a stiff neck and was glad to wrap the khaif up in her towel and lay it in the corner of the kitchen. Then somehow she must live through the long hours of the day until the lights began to twinkle in the streets and she could run up the magic staircase and see the four candles burning and lay her gift at the feet of the Baby.

She kept wondering if the Baby had arrived yet and once or twice she tiptoed to the passage and listened furtively for the sound of happy cooing or contented chuckling. But all was quiet and the door where the little girl lived was tight shut, so it did not trouble her much. Perhaps the Baby was coming by ship and they had all gone down to the port to meet him. The sun shone in wintry gleams on the water, breaking through the clouds and showing glimpses of the coast of Spain across the Straits, and Europeans smiled gaily and said that it would be fine for Christmas after all.

Twilight – the crowded Boulevards a blaze of colour and light – because all the shops were open on Christmas Eve, Sunday or no Sunday. Aisha's mother was busy as usual in the yard and Fatima had disappeared. Aisha was all alone in the kitchen and the moment had obviously arrived to go and look for the Baby. Even now they would surely be lighting the fourth candle. Hope, love, fear, courage, awe and longing, all flooded her simple little heart like a great tide, and drove her breathless into the dark passage, clasping the precious khaif tightly against her chest.

She tiptoed to the bottom of the staircase and looked up. The door was once more ajar and the soft welcoming light streamed towards her – a little stronger and clearer than before because tomorrow would be Christmas and Petra had lit all four Advent candles in honour of the Festival.

It was very quiet. Perhaps the Baby was asleep. Aisha, rosy with joy, scuttled up the staircase towards her fairyland.

But as she reached the top of the stairs a rough hand shot out and seized her by the arm, and too bewildered to cry out she found she was being hustled downstairs; slapped and shaken, stumbling and gasping, she was at the bottom before she was really aware of what had happened, and then the light from the kitchen shone on Fatima's furious face so terrifyingly near her own.

'Yes, I know all about it,' snarled Fatima, who dared not make too much noise in the passage. 'Zohra told me – sneaking upstairs right into my lady's room; I thought I'd just catch you at it tonight – you try that again – this is the end of you – I'll tell your mother of you.' – Slap! slap!

Aisha, coming to her senses, gave a loud scream. Fatima clapped her hand over her mouth, pushed her through the front door and slammed it behind her. She was alone on the steps, still clasping her khaif to her heart.

She had no idea where she was going, but she must get away somehow from the terrible Fatima, and she started running down the gay Boulevards, bumping into the people, noticing nothing, sobbing bitterly. But it was not the slapping or shaking that she really minded – in fact she hardly thought about them at all. What really mattered was, she had not seen the Baby. She had crept within a few yards of Him; without a doubt He had been there, fast asleep in a soft cradle, lapped in the light of four candles, but the khaif that was to have been laid reverently on His quilt was still in her hand.

She was so lost in grief that she never heard the people shout or the policeman blow his whistle or the scream of brakes as she dashed blindly across the road. Nor could she ever remember afterwards being knocked over by the big car. She lay unconscious in the road and the crowds gathered round her, all chattering in different languages, until the ambulance arrived and drove her to the English hospital on the cliff overlooking the Straits of Gibraltar.

The Baby

She did not wake properly till twilight the next day because she had struck her head on the kerb and concussed herself slightly; also her leg had been broken by the wheel of the car. She half woke during the afternoon, and thought she heard the sound of singing very far away and thought she saw candles burning: but it might all have been a dream.

But when she woke at dusk she knew quite well she was not dreaming. She was wide awake and her leg hurt her and she felt giddy, but where she was she could not imagine. After a while she gave up trying to imagine and just lay quite still, looking and listening.

She was lying on a raised bedstead, which was

slightly alarming because she had never slept anywhere but on the floor. However, there was a whole row of other people on raised bedsteads and they did not appear to be falling out so perhaps it was quite safe after all. At the other end of the room there were groups of people all looking at a tree, and among the evergreen branches burned, not four candles, but many, many candles all different colours; under the boughs stood a row of children in long, bright silk dresses, singing in Arabic –

'Away in a manger, no crib for His bed,
The little Lord Jesus lay down His sweet head.'

Aisha's heart gave a sudden leap. 'The little Lord Jesus' – that was the name of the Baby who was going to stay with Petra, but apparently He was here instead, for they were singing about Him and had lit at least fifty candles in honour of His coming. All other events were still confused and blurred, but Petra, the Baby, and the four candles were all perfectly clear in her mind.

She fell asleep again and when she woke it was night and there were no candles – only one tiny red lamp glowing above the door, casting a dim light over the room. Nor was there any more singing – only the snoring of sleeping patients. Aisha lifted her head cautiously from her pillow and looked round. The night nurse noticed her and came over to see how she was feeling.

Aisha liked nurses. Just a year ago the youngest baby but one had accidentally sat down in the clay bowl of red-hot charcoal and Aisha had carried him to this same hospital every morning for his dressings. The nurse had always been kind and pleased to see her and once she had checked Absalom's yells with a pink sweet. Nurses were definitely friendly and trustworthy. Aisha smiled and kissed this one's hand by way of greeting.

'I want to see the Baby!' said Aisha. 'Where is He? Has He gone to sleep yet?'

'Which baby?' asked the nurse gently. 'Do you mean your baby brother?'

'No, I don't,' answered Aisha, 'I mean the Baby called Jesus. He was going to Petra's house and then He came here instead. The children sang about Him and all the candles were lit. Where is He? . . . I had a present for Him but I don't know where it is now.'

The nurse was puzzled. How had this little Moslem child with her big anxious black eyes heard of the Blessed Babe? And who was Petra? She sat down on Aisha's bed and tried to explain.

'Aisha,' she said, 'you cannot see the Baby Jesus because He was born many years ago and now He has gone back to God. But the children were keeping the Feast of His birthday and singing how He came into the world to save us from sin and sadness. I'll tell you about Him, Aisha, and then you'll understand.'

Aisha lay very still, her black eyes fixed on the nurse's face. She wanted to understand about the Baby more than anything else in the world.

'God loved us, Aisha,' said the nurse, 'so He sent His Son the Lord Jesus to show us the way to Heaven. He became a little baby like us. His mother was very poor and laid Him in a manger when He was born. He has gone back to God now, but He is still alive and He still loves us. He is with us all the time although we can't see Him and He can still show us the way to Heaven.'

She shook up the child's pillow and moved away noiselessly, and Aisha lay staring at the red glow of the tiny lamp, thinking, thinking.

She had imagined herself running into the love-light of that candle glow for one moment, flinging her gift at the feet of the Baby, and then running back into the cold dark for ever. Now it was all different. He was not coming after all, and she would never see Him; yet she was not unhappy, for the nurse had told her something even better.

'He loves you. He is with you all the time although you can't see Him. . . . He will show you the way to Heaven.' That was what the nurse had said, and half-asleep and half-awake she fancied she saw a long bright road winding away through the darkness. At the beginning of the road stood the Baby, beautiful and rosy, tousled and bright-eyed as though newly awakened from sleep. In one hand He clasped a lighted candle and with the other He beckoned to her to follow Him, and the love of his happy heart drew her irresistibly just as the glow of light had drawn her up the dark stairway. In her dream she ran to Him and put her hand into His and knew that she had found everything she had ever wanted in her life and that nothing need ever frighten her or hurt her again, because no one could take the Baby from her or her from the Baby. And in the presence of the Baby there was safety and love and shelter and fulness of joy.

When All the Candles Were Lit

Aisha's leg was broken quite badly and she stayed in hospital six weeks and enjoyed every moment of it. But the highlights of the day were at three o'clock in the afternoon when her mother came to visit her, with the baby tied on her back and all the little brothers and sisters trailing behind, and seven o'clock at night when the English missionary appeared with a portable harmonium and they all sang hymns and heard wonderful stories about what happened to the Baby when He grew up.

She loved hearing how He laid His hands on sick people and made them better without any medicine at all, and on little children and sent them away happy and good and blessed, and on a dead little girl about Aisha's age who had sat up at once and felt hungry. But one night the English missionary told a very sad story of how those kind hands had been nailed to a cross of wood, and the Lord Jesus had been put to death. He had died willingly and lovingly to pay for all the wrong things that Aisha and everyone else in the world had done, and this made Aisha very sorry for she knew that she had very, very often told lies and lost her temper and been rude to her mother and slapped the babies. She lay thinking about it far into the night and once again she half dreamed, half imagined that the Baby came and held out His little hands to her and this time she could see that they had been wounded; and she knew that all the wrong things she had done could be forgiven and she could start all over again, with a heart washed clean and white.

'All my life I am going to follow the Baby in the path that leads to God,' she whispered, clasping her small brown hands. She loved Him with all her heart and longed to give Him a gift. She thought of beautiful little Petra lighting candles for His Coming and wrapping up presents. She wished she too could light candles – but she couldn't. She was just a poor, dark, common child with nothing to give.

After a time she was presented with some crutches and allowed to leap around the garden, then she was allowed to walk alone with a stick – and one beautiful spring day when the happy winds were ruffling the waves into sparkling foam, and puffing through the open ward window, the doctor told Aisha he was going to take her home that afternoon in his car.

She lay quietly thinking about it after he had gone. She couldn't be quite sure if she was pleased or not. It was not that she was saying goodbye altogether, because she was coming back to Sunday school every week and bringing

Safea with her to visit all the nurses; but six weeks is a long time in the life of a little girl and she had become used to order, cleanliness and space, and all these things were entirely lacking in the shack up the mountain. She thought of the goat, the babies, the cats, the overturned buckets of water, the charcoal smoke, the leaking roof on wet days and the washing that wouldn't dry, and she sighed a little. When the nurse asked her if she wasn't excited, she didn't answer.

The doctor arrived directly after dinner and hustled her off with the voices of the patients ringing in her ears. 'Visit us again, Aisha – go in peace and may God bring you to happiness!' She was unencumbered by any luggage and waved to them with both hands as the car sped out of the gate. Then they were roaring up the mountain road, and the sea through the dip in the hills was far below them and the town far behind them.

The doctor, who had visits further up the mountain, set her down on the slope below her home and bade her goodbye, and for a few moments she stood there alone looking about her. The narcissi were out along the stream bed and black baby lambs gambolled among stretches of blue wild iris. The wind came sweeping up from the sea and, as though it had carried the whisper of her home-coming in its wings, the children suddenly saw her and came tumbling out of the cottage to meet her.

The next few minutes were just a bewildering jumble of shouts and laughter and hugs and kisses, but somehow she found herself sitting on the cottage steps with the baby on her lap, Absalom behind her with his arms clasped tightly round her neck, Mustapha and Sodea, one under each arm, beaming up at her; the goat butted her rather painfully in the back, her mother made mint tea in honour of her homecoming, and Safea stood in front of her on one leg, her slim little body swaying like the mimosa tree in the wind in her ecstasy of joy.

And Aisha, flushed and gloriously happy, suddenly laughed out loud as she remembered the quite clean hospital ward and her lovely white bed. She wondered how she had borne living for six weeks away from the hot tight little arms, and the grubby sticky hands of the little brothers and sisters. She looked down at the thin baby with its spotty head and running nose and decided there had never been another child equal to it for beauty and dearness. Her heart was almost bursting with a new awareness of love for them all, and she suddenly remembered and understood why.

She had come to know the other Baby – He was living in her heart, the fountain of all love and gentleness and joy. He was there beside her, shedding His light over the spring hillside, the cottage, the mother and the grimy happy faces of the children, and she saw everything in its blessed glow.

The Heavenly Babe Himself had lit the candles.

The Cloak

Morning

The grey light was stealing into the city streets when Mustapha awoke, shivered and pulled his ragged old cloak tightly round him. His face was covered by the hood, but he pushed it back just a little and peered round. He wanted to see what was happening but he didn't want to let in the draughts.

The other boys lay round, sleeping uneasily. Their lodging was a café in an evil street, and the air was still thick with last night's stale tobacco smoke. Dirty glasses stood on the tables and the boys were unwashed and homeless. Most of them lay huddled up as though conscious of the cold, and some muttered a little at the pale light.

Mustapha stared at them gloomily from under his hood. He had not been long in the city and he hated the daily chilly awakening in this wretched place. It was not comfortable sleeping on the floor, but he was used to that, and at least in sleep you could forget that you were hungry and dirty and outcast. Sometimes in his dreams he drifted back to the time, not so long ago, when he had lain down at night beside his mother in their mountain home, and the folds of her dress had kept him warm. He must have been dreaming about her that morning, for while he was still only half awake he found himself thinking about her; she was an ignorant tribeswoman but her love for him had been very strong. How often she had given him bread and gone hungry herself; perhaps that was partly why she had died so young. It was three years since he had seen the mountains near her home and he wondered what they looked like now – probably all under snow, with the gales tearing down the ravines. It was warmer in the city, but the mountain air had been clean and untainted. He suddenly wrinkled his nose, got up with an expression of disgust, and made his way stiffly to the door. He had paid for his lodging the night before and had nothing to do but to go.

The cold air of the street seemed to hit him and he trotted along fast, his teeth chattering. It was only 6 a.m., but oh, how he wanted some breakfast! From the Mosque nearby came the dawn prayer call, but Mustapha had never learned to pray. He had nowhere to go and nothing to do, and with his dream of the mountains fresh in his mind the streets seemed unbearable.

He would go down to the beach; there at least he would find clean breezes and wide spaces, and there he could run and get warm. He pattered down a broader alley with shuttered shops on each side; at the bottom was a wharf and a stone jetty running out to the port where big ships rode at anchor, but away to the right stretched the long, curved sands of the bay, bounded by scrubby hills. And over the waters of the bay and the lighthouse on the headland the sky was aflame with sunrise. Even the sullen boy was struck by its beauty and stood wondering for a moment. It was so lonely. Just himself and the wheeling gulls and the little crisp waves tinted with gold.

Then his eyes, sharp with hunger, caught sight of something else. Far away, on the beach across the bay, a fishing boat was moored and some men were coming down to the margin of the sea in a group. Mustapha knew what that meant – a net to be pulled in. He might get his breakfast yet! Slipping off his cloak he girded himself with it, and began running along the firm sands, the gulls rising up in front of him screaming, his bare feet leaving a track on the tide-washed stretches.

He arrived panting to find them all in rather a bad mood. They had been quarrelling over the division of the price of the haul, and two boys had gone off in a rage refusing to work. Mustapha had arrived in the nick of time.

'I'll pull with you,' he panted, drawing himself up straight, 'and help you carry it up to market.'

His tone was a little too eager. The fisherman recognized that the boy was desperate for work and would probably take anything. He mentioned a very small sum; Mustapha's eyes flashed.

'It's too little,' he protested angrily.

'All right, you can clear out,' replied the fisherman, rolling up his sleeves. 'There are other boys about.'

There were, too. Already they were scudding along the beach and Mustapha had to decide quickly. He must either accept such meanness or go hungry. Scowling with rage he flung his old cloak on the sands and took his place at the tarry rope. The other men fell into line and at a word from the fisherman they all hauled together.

The drawing in of a net is a beautiful sight. Men, boys and little half-naked children strain backwards, the muscles of their brown limbs taut and rippling, their heels digging deep into the sand. Then, as one man, they all relax and clasp the rope further down before the next great pull. They work in silence, to a perfect rhythm, adding their little strength to the might of the incoming tide, and the net, far out at sea, is borne to the shore. Then, with a last great heave and a sudden shout, the net is landed and a frenzied mass of silver fish writhes on the sand, sparkling in the sunshine, while the men run forward to examine and sort the catch. Much of it is no good, and is thrown on one side in a bright heap of red starfish and orange jelly-fish; but the sardines, the octopuses, the herrings and the mackerels are piled into flat wooden boxes which drip at the joints, and the boys carry them on bowed shoulders to market, their clothes becoming soaked with salt fishy water.

Mustapha lost no time in seizing a box of sardines, for other boys were eager for the job as well as himself. In fact, they were quarrelling already and he deemed it better to go as soon as possible. He set off at a steady trot, the cold water leaking down his neck; but he was happy, for he had not long now to wait for his breakfast and he wanted his breakfast more than anything else on earth.

It was quite a climb to the market, and his shoulders ached and his fingers were numb. But the market was full these days, for it was the season when the Christians celebrated the birth of Christ and all ate turkey and cakes and bought flowers and toys for their children. The flower stalls in the centre of the square were a blaze of colour; blue irises massed against yellow mimosa and fragrant bunches of narcissus, and backed by dark boughs of fir and little potted Christmas trees. The meat market was a sight, too, for all the turkeys and geese and chickens had red paper frills round their necks. And the crowds! It was only eight o'clock in the morning, but already the streets were thronged with French, Spanish and English shoppers with big baskets on their arms making their last bargains. For tomorrow was Christmas.

Mustapha dumped the fish before its owner and received his payment with a scowl. It should have been far more than that; the man was a cheat and a robber of the poor! Still, Mustapha was used to that, and the coin would buy him breakfast, four fried dough rings for a peseta and a glass of coffee. He would feel better after that and he would spend the morning in the market in hopes of carrying a Christmas basket for some overladen housewife. The day began to look brighter except that his damp garment clung to him, and there was very little warmth in the winter sunshine. Where was his old cloak?

He suddenly remembered. He'd left it on the beach. In his haste to get away, and warm with the exercise of pulling and carrying, he had forgotten all about it.

He forgot his hunger, for to lose his cloak was about the worst thing that could happen to him. Turning his back on the market he scudded down the streets as fast as he could and reached the sea front. Now he was on the shore again, running, running. The tide had come in, and the river that flowed into the sea had filled up and was quite deep. He plunged in almost up to his waist, but hardly noticed the cold for the thought of his loss made him forget everything else. Eagerly he scanned the beach; yes, that was the place. There was the boat and the useless heap of jelly-fish and the sand churned up by their feet. But the cloak had gone.

Yes, it had gone and it was no use searching any more. He was warm with running now, but he had to get back across the river and soon he would be frozen. There was no hope of getting another and the cold weather was just beginning. He'd have to save up for a sack and he'd better save up in good earnest, too. He would start by going without his coffee and making do with two dough rings.

Bitterly angry, he wandered back towards the town. The sun was high now, and the sea a sheet of sparkling blue. The coast of Spain across the Straits was hidden by a silver haze. Why was the morning so beautiful, and men so wicked? He had been cheated of half his wages. His cloak had been stolen. He hated everybody.

Midday

The packet-boat from Gibraltar arrived at 11 a.m., and as it came round the headland Mustapha hurried down the stone jetty that led to the Port so as to get there in good time. This was usually the best hour of his day, the hour on which he depended for his dinner. The thing was to be there early, for there were many other hungry ragamuffins who also depended on the Gibraltar Packet for their dinner and there wasn't always enough work to go round.

With the scream of sirens and the rush of steam, and the thrashing of a backward revolving propeller, the ship drew in and cast anchor. Every boy was alert and on his toes then as the passengers streamed through the Customs with heavy cases, or better still, as heavy cargo was piled on the wharf to be lifted on to lorries. As far as passengers were concerned, the game was to attach yourself to the greenest, most bewildered-looking tourist, preferably an American, as they had the most money, and offer to show him round the town, or take him to a hotel for a fabulous price. The art was to appear so charming that the tourist would be unable to believe that anyone so considerate and anxious for his welfare could be capable of cheating him. But if this failed, there were usually cases to carry.

Mustapha was not much good at the tourist trade. He was too thin, and his dark eyes were too sad. Besides, years of mountain solitude had left him unsure of himself in crowds. Tourists had not come to be reminded of poverty and hunger. They had come to enjoy themselves and they liked jolly, amusing, self-confident boys. Still, he did occasionally get a catch and today he pranced up to a young lady in shorts, slung about with binoculars and camera – obviously over for the day and most uncertain of herself. She was silly to come alone and should be easy prey.

'I show you all,' he chanted, airing the three stock sentences of English that he knew, gambolling about a little in a desperate effort to be jolly and amusing, 'I very good. Hundred pesetas.'

The girl hesitated and might have fallen into the trap. But a fat man, smoking a big cheroot cigar, came to her rescue.

'Not a cent more than twenty, young lady,' he remarked firmly, 'and if I were you, I should get a proper guide. These boys are thieves and rascals.'

The girl stalked off with an indignant look at Mustapha, who stood scowling. He hated the fat man in the fur-lined overcoat, with his cheroot cigar. What did he know about hunger? There he was, taking the girl off himself, probably to some expensive restaurant up on the Boulevard to gorge and drink and smoke. However, it was no good wasting time brooding. He must look sharp or he'd get nothing. There was a tired-looking Spanish woman with a baby and a heavy suitcase, the type who could not afford a taxi; not very profitable, but there was nothing else left. He must screw all he could out of her. He rushed forward and seized the case. She gave it up and he hurried along the wharf with it, casting angry envious glances at a friend of his who had got hold of an expensive-looking young man in a brilliant tie and was making him laugh! Make 'em laugh and they'd hand out anything. That boy would get a good dinner.

He hadn't gone five yards before a man came running down the wharf and kissed the tired woman and took the baby in his arms. Then he reached out for the suitcase and dropped two pesetas into Mustapha's outstretched hand without looking at him; and it was no use arguing or making a row, because it was all that was reasonably due to him and anyhow the husband and wife were far too interested in each other to take any notice of him.

The big chance of his day was over, and he'd earned two pesetas.

He loafed along the beach, sick of everything and watching the waves. It was midday. He had no heart left to rush straight back to the milling market. He would wait a little. The beach, if you walked on past the footballers, was the only quiet place in the town, and Mustapha sometimes hungered for quietness. The city was a cruel place where every man lived flat out for himself and the strongest and the most cunning came out on top. He suddenly longed to turn his back on it all and go back to the rocks and rivers of his tribal village. But his father and mother were dead, and there was no place for him there – nor anywhere else, he thought, staring dully at the sea.

He had reached the spot where they had hauled in the net that morning. The boat still lay on its side on the beach and a dark-eyed boy with a shaved head was sitting cross-legged on the sand, mending a net. When he noticed Mustapha he stared at him intently.

'Were you on the net, this morning?' he asked.

'Yes,' replied Mustapha, disinterestedly.

'So was I,' said the boy, 'I saw you. Did you lose your cloak?'

'Yes,' answered Mustapha, suddenly eager. 'Where is it?'

The boy threw a pebble in the air and caught it. He was silent for a moment.

'What will you give me, if I tell you?' he asked cautiously.

Mustapha felt desperate. 'I have nothing to give you,' he cried. 'I haven't had any dinner yet, and the fisherman cheated me over my wages. Tell me where it is and I'll pay you another day.'

The fisher lad shook his head shrewdly. It was a land where no boy would trust another boy.

'One peseta,' he bargained, 'and I'll show you the house. The man who stole it has gone out with the boats and won't be home for a couple of days. There's only a woman there. You can just take it. I live next door and I saw him carry it off.'

He went quietly on with his work without looking up. There was no moving him. Mustapha flung the peseta down on the sand beside him, and the boy gathering up the net rose to his feet.

'Come on,' he said, 'follow me!'

They hurried up the beach and over the railway line and across the road to the salt meadows. There sea water was stored in hollows and ditches, and as it evaporated under the scorching summer sun the deposit of salt was left behind. But in the winter the meadows were dry and the only signs of life were a few ragged children playing round a cluster of black tarry huts, where fishermen and salt-makers lived.

'That's it,' said the boy very quietly, giving a

nod towards the smallest hut. 'Good-bye, and may God help you!'

He disappeared into his own home and Mustapha hesitated a moment. He felt rather frightened, but anger made him bold. Marching to the door he knocked loudly and stuck out his chest, in an effort to look manly.

There was silence for a moment. Then a weak voice said, 'Come in.'

It was a very bare room and rather dark. In one corner lay a pile of fishing tackle and a baby donkey, and in the other lay a girl on a straw mat hugging a clay pot of ashes and moaning a little. A neighbour sat beside her and at their feet tossed a restless little figure covered with Mustapha's cloak.

Ha! The boy had spoken the truth. This was the den of thieves and now he had caught them! He would seize his cloak and threaten them with the police till they cried for mercy. Not that he intended to carry out his threat, for Mustapha's whole life was spent avoiding the police, and it would be a great mistake to have anything to do with them. Still, it would sound good.

'Where's the man who stole my cloak?' he shouted gruffly, trying to disguise the childish break in his voice. 'You'd better hand it over quickly and pay me for having taken it, or the police will be here in half an hour. Do you hear me?'

The young woman turned her head wearily.

She seemed to be thinking of something else. Mustapha realized that he had made very little impression and his loud, gruff voice sounded foolish and cheap. His boasting was quite lost on the tired mother and the sick child, for they had neither the heart nor the strength to resist him, had they wanted to. The neighbour, a worn old granny, just stared at him, for it was none of her business. Only the baby donkey seemed frightened and backed into its corner. Mustapha was sorry about that, for he had been brought up with a baby donkey.

'Take it,' said the young woman, lifting her head and pointing to the little heap at her feet. 'My husband has gone out with the boats. He won't be home till tomorrow night. I have no money in the house.'

She turned her face to the wall and shut her eyes. There was nothing left to do but to take it. It was an abject victory. He dragged it defiantly off the child who cried out and shivered, as though woken suddenly from a restless dream. Even Mustapha could see that it was a very sick child. The old neighbour rose up slowly, every joint creaking, and carried the feverish mite to its mother's side and laid it under the cotton wrap that covered her. Perhaps her arms would keep it warm.

No one spoke. There was nothing to do but to go away. As he left the cottage, the cloak over his arm, a cold cloud blew across the sun and dark shadows brooded on the sea.

Back along the beach; he was feeling almost faint with hunger now and strangely miserable. Usually his feelings were perfectly simple. If he came out top he was happy and if someone else came out top he was unhappy, and as he was only a country boy, not very sharp or cunning, and no match for city urchins, he was usually unhappy. But today he had won, hands down, and he was wretched; he wondered why.

Afternoon

He bought a hunk of bread and two fried sardines and looked round for a social spot to eat it in. He did not want to be alone. He wanted noise and company, loud racy talk and perhaps a fight – anything to make him forget the quiet room, the tarry smell of fishing tackle, the white-faced woman and the sick child. He joined a group of boot-blacks and café assistants lounging on the pavement by the bus stop, and sat down to enjoy his dinner as best he could.

The boot-blacks were doing well, for everyone wanted to be smart for Christmas. They had been up in the market and were full of tall stories, for this Feast was an interesting time of year – so much food in the shop windows and a certain amount of generosity in the hearts of buyers.

'What do these Christians *do* at this feast of theirs?' asked one lanky boy contemptuously.

'They eat turkey,' replied a scruffy-looking

man. 'I used to work for one of them. And they get drunk too, and smoke many, many cigars, and give presents to their children. It was a wonder how much they ate! But they didn't offer me any. I was only the gardener's boy.'

He spat contemptuously and lounged against the wall.

'And *why* do they keep this feast?' asked the lanky boy again. He seemed interested.

'They say it's the day their prophet Jesus was born,' replied another lad. 'They say He is the Son of God. Lies and blasphemy! May God preserve all faithful Moslems!'

'I know all about it,' chipped in a third lad eagerly. 'I've been in the Christian hospital. I had a fight with a chap who stole my tobacco and he knifed me in the shoulder. I stayed in their hospital four days and at night they came and preached their religion and taught us wicked words. This is what they tried to make us learn: "God so loved the world that He gave His only begotten Son."'

He mimicked the voice of the foreign speaker perfectly and his performance was greeted with a roar of laughter.

'The good Moslems get under the bedclothes,' went on the speaker, much encouraged, 'but some listen and even repeat the words because they think they'll get better treatment. Hypocrites! However, I must say that doctor was kind. He treated us all alike whether we listened or not, and he made no favourites of the rich.'

An older man, who had been chewing gum thoughtfully while he listened, suddenly broke in.

'Not all are hypocrites,' he remarked. 'Just now and again one is deceived and believes. There was that boy Hassan who worked at the port. He was in that hospital for two months with typhoid and they bewitched him good and proper. . . . He said he wasn't a Moslem any longer. He lost his job, and his family turned him out, but nothing would move him. And the strange thing was that he never shouted back at them or argued – just went quietly on; said he'd found the way of peace.'

'And where is he now?' enquired the former gardener's boy.

'I don't know. He begged in the streets for a while, but no Moslem would help him. Anyhow, he's no longer of our company. Poor fool!'

The talk moved on to other subjects. The boot-blacks returned to the market, but Mustapha and a few others lingered on, for a long-distance bus would be coming soon and then there might be work for one or two of them. The afternoon was drawing on. The ex-gardener put his hand in his pocket and gave a loud exclamation. His pocket had been picked.

Furiously he set on the nearest boy, who happened to be Mustapha. The lad struggled, but his cloak was dragged off his back, and he was cuffed into silence while they searched him. Finding him innocent they pushed him aside and made off to find a policeman to round up the boot-blacks.

What a fight and commotion there'd be! Mustapha, bruised and shaken, decided to get as far away as possible. He made for his one and only refuge, the seashore, and for the third time that day he paced the margin of the waves, sick at heart.

For a long time he did not look up. What a miserable day it had been! All days weren't like that. Some days the sun shone; they laughed and joked and managed to make money, and then there was food and keep. But, come to think of it, they nearly always laughed because someone had been hurt or cheated or robbed. Today, on that deserted stretch of beach, Mustapha suddenly seemed to see things as they were, and hated all the greed and malice and fear and quarrelling and uncleanness that made up their daily lives. Tired and bruised, he flung himself down on the sand and stared at the sea.

He looked up. The soft colours of the sky were reflected in the water. A gull rose towards the last light on shining wings. Why had they spoiled the world like this? And was there any escape from such a rotten existence? He did not know. He had never really thought about it before.

Then he suddenly remembered fragments of the conversation by the bus stop. He remembered quite clearly because they used words he so seldom heard. 'God so loved that He gave . . . he said he had found a way of peace!'

Loving . . . giving . . . peace. Like three bright signposts in a wilderness, these words seemed scrawled across the rosy sky; words that, as yet, meant almost nothing to Mustapha and his gang. Hating, grabbing, fighting – that was their code; but it did not lead to any way of peace.

And yet Mustapha had known about these words in years past. His mother had loved him and given, given, given until she had nothing left at all. And Mustapha remembered that she had lain down at peace on the night she died. It was snowing, and she had wrapped him in the only warm covering in the house. It was the last she had to give.

What was *peace*? Early summer mornings on the mountains, sunset over the sea . . . loving . . . giving. But he had frightened a helpless woman and stripped the covering from a sick child. Suddenly, quite clearly, he knew where his own path of peace lay and he turned his head to look at it. The stretches of water in the salt flats looked blood-red in the last light, and the boats rose up like black silhouettes against the sunset.

He got up like someone in a dream and crossed the railway line and the trenched meadows. The door of the fisherman's hut was not locked, for the neighbour was returning later and had left it on the latch. Mustapha opened it very softly without knocking and stepped inside.

A little lamp was burning and all was quiet save for the laboured breathing of the child –

but Mustapha knew at once that something had happened. The young woman was propped up on a pillow looking down at the new baby she held at her breast, and her tired face was utterly peaceful, for she too was loving and giving.

It must have been born soon after Mustapha left, for the room was clean and tidy, the baby washed, and the mother had slept and woken again. The little donkey had drawn close and stood watching on long wobbly legs, and the sick child tossed and moaned under the cotton covering. Then the woman suddenly looked up and saw Mustapha standing shyly in the doorway.

She gave a cry of fear and would have beaten on the wall to call her neighbour, but Mustapha ran forward.

'Don't be afraid,' he said, 'I'm not going to hurt you. I came to lend you my cloak – just for tonight, because your child is ill. Tomorrow I must take it back, but I'll try and bring you a sack. Tonight, in any case, she shall sleep warm.'

He stooped and covered the little girl, and the woman looked at him very curiously. When he had come before he had stuck out his chest and shouted and swaggered like a man, but now as he stood there, humble and deflated, she realized that he was only a young boy, fourteen at the most, a mere child, not yet quite hardened to wickedness.

'Sit down,' she said in a weak voice, 'the teapot is on the fire. Pour yourself out a glass.'

51

He huddled over the dying charcoal and drank a glass of hot, sweet mint tea with relish. It was days since he'd tasted any.

'Why did you bring it back?' asked the woman, still very puzzled.

'*Hakada*,' replied Mustapha, which is a convenient way of saying, 'What is, is, but I couldn't give any reason for it if I tried.' As a matter of fact he couldn't understand himself what had made him do such a thing.

'Where do you live?' went on the woman.

'Nowhere,' answered the boy. 'I've only been here three years. I came down from the tribes.'

'Why, so did I,' said the woman eagerly. 'My husband brought me down when I married him seven years ago and I've never been back since. What village do you come from?'

Mustapha named his village. It was only a few miles from hers on the eastern side of the same mountain. They had travelled the same paths to market, picked olives on the same slopes, and burned charcoal among the same rocks. She was too tired to talk much, but he poured out his homesick heart to this alien sister of his, for in three years she was the first person he had met who knew his village.

He talked of spring, with its swollen streams and foaming cherry and apricot blossom – of summer, when they cut the harvests and slept on the threshing floors – of autumn, when they gathered figs and grapes and Indian corn cobs, and spread them out to dry on the baked cactus in front of the huts – of winter, when the villages were snow-bound and the cattle lived indoors. He was back again in thought on his mountain, a happy child, running up the rocks after the goats, and coming home to his mother at night. He talked and talked, and she lay and listened, occasionally asking a few questions. But she was not as homesick as he was, for her children had been born in the hut on the salt flat and that anchored her heart fast. Home to her was the baby in her arms and the child who lay tossing at her feet.

It gave a sudden sharp cry, and the mother dragged herself painfully forward to quieten it. It had woken and wanted water. She held a glass to its lips and it drank feverishly and wept with little gasping sobs to come into her arms. She laid the new baby on the floor and dragged the sick child towards her.

'What is the matter with it?' asked Mustapha.

'I don't know,' answered the woman, rocking it wearily to and fro. 'It has been ill three days. Each day I ask my husband to take it to the hospital, but he does not love it, because he wanted a boy, and he always says he hasn't time. I am too weak to go, so I suppose she will die, but if I could carry her to the doctor she would live.'

'How do you know?' asked Mustapha.

'I took her before,' explained the woman simply. 'She had fever as she has now, and could neither suck nor draw breath. The doctor gave her the needle and her fever went away. He would do it again, for he is a kind man, but who can carry her? We have no money to ask him to come here.'

Mustapha thought for a moment. Then he said, 'I will carry her. I know where the hospital is.'

The woman looked at him as though weighing him up. She was an ignorant woman who knew very little about sickness, and she was desperately afraid her child would die. She did not like sending it out by night in the cold, but she had unbounded faith in the needle and thought this was probably its only chance. As for Mustapha, the fact that he came from her district made her trust him as she would have trusted a kinsman.

The little girl, finding herself at last where she had longed to be all day, safe in her mother's arms, had fallen fast asleep and did not wake when Mustapha picked her up. They wrapped her in the cloak, and nodding goodbye he set off across the flats at a quick pace. The moon was coming up over the sea, making a silver track across the waves, and Mustapha was glad of its light for he had quite a long way to go. The child lay with her head on his shoulder and the pressure of her burning little body kept him warm. He took the short cut back along the beach; the tide was out and the stretches of sand were moon-washed and glistening. There was no one else about at all, just he and his little burden; once or twice she stirred and whimpered but he soothed her and rocked her a little, and whispered tender words learned long ago and almost forgotten. 'If only she gets better!' he thought.

He had almost reached the pier now, and must cut straight up through the town. The market would be grand tonight, a blaze of noise and colour, but Mustapha had no wish to leave the beach. Here on the silver sands he felt peaceful, as though there was healing and forgiveness in the Christmas moonlight.

He did not know why he felt peaceful. He had hardly noticed that he, Mustapha, was loving and giving.

Evening

Oh yes, the market on Christmas Eve was a gay sight, the stalls glittering with lighted Christmas trees and shop windows blazing. The place swarmed with prosperous children out for walks in their best clothes and seeing the sights with their parents – also with wretched beggars, some blind and deformed, hoping to profit from the general lavishness. Mustapha's friends were all there too, and on any other night Mustapha would have been among them enjoying the fun, and flat out for what he could snatch. But tonight he had an errand and he did not want to meet his friends. He chose the more deserted back streets and hurried on past the town centre up the cobbled steps that led to the top of the cliff, where stood the hospital.

He had some misgivings about this doctor. From all accounts he might well be celebrating with the rest, or even drunk. Mustapha was rather weak from insufficient food and the hot baby in his arms seemed to grow heavier and heavier. He hoped he had not come for nothing.

He had reached the double gates that led to the hospital compound and he hesitated, wondering which way to go. There seemed to be several big lighted buildings and a bewildering number of doors. Then, as he stood wondering, a man of his own race crossed the garden between the houses and Mustapha, taking his courage in both hands, went up to him and asked timidly for the doctor.

'He's in the house,' said the man, jerking his thumb over his shoulder, 'but he's busy.'

'But this little girl is very ill,' faltered the boy. 'I've brought her a long way.'

The man glanced at her and heard the laboured breathing. He shrugged his shoulders. 'You'd better go and see,' he said. 'Knock at the door and show him the child.'

Mustapha crept on. The door of the house was shut, but light streamed from the windows and there was the sound of music and laughter from within. The boy hesitated. No doubt they were celebrating, and perhaps they would all be drunk after all. But no; as he listened he realized that the sounds he had heard were the laughter and shouting of little children. Perhaps, after all, a little child would be welcome here.

So he knocked and stood ready for flight should things turn out badly.

The doctor himself opened the door; he looked flushed and his hair was standing on end, but he was not drunk. He had merely been playing musical chairs and he carried his own fat, rosy son of three in his arms.

He stood blinking at Mustapha for a moment, his eyes unaccustomed to the darkness. He saw a boy, with a white, hungry, dirty face and dull eyes, very thin and dressed in a cotton garment that had once been white; and in his arms he carried an unwholesome-looking baby wrapped in a ragged cloak.

'It's ill,' said Mustapha, and held it out.

The doctor, who was also a father, put his own son down in the passage, and it toddled off to rejoin the party in the room on the left. Then he stretched out his arms and took in its place the other baby, thin, dirty, and sick, and carried it into the warmth and light of his own home. Years later when Mustapha had become a Christian he often remembered that moment, for to him it embodied the whole meaning of Christmas. A father – a son – the dark night outside – and the needy outcast welcomed in.

The doctor fetched some things from his study and then sat down in the passage and listened to the child's chest with a strange tube. He took its temperature, which made it scream and reach out for Mustapha, to whom it had taken a liking. It was ill, but not as ill as the mother had feared; just a very bad cold and a touch of bronchitis. He would take it across to the hospital, and nurse would give it the needle that Mustapha had tremblingly suggested, and then it could go home again. He told Mustapha to wait in the passage till he returned.

Mustapha sat quietly listening to the noise within and wondering where all these children came from. Surely they could not all belong to the doctor! Never before had he heard little children laugh so much or sound so happy. Then someone came out and he craned his neck to get a glimpse inside, and what he saw surprised him. For they were mostly children of his own race – little girls in long dresses and dark plaits, and little boys with shaved heads and baggy trousers, all eating cake. He had not known that the Christians shared their feast with Moslem children.

Quick steps outside and the doctor returned with a howling baby. Mustapha bowed and kissed his hand, and held out his arms for his little charge, who cast herself into them and re-lapsed into snuffles and hiccoughs. He must get back quickly.

But the doctor had not quite finished. He saw a great deal of poverty every day, but seldom had he seen anything as pinched and wretched-look-ing as this boy. And it was Christmas Eve.

'Just a moment,' he said. 'She'll need another tomorrow. Where does she live?'

'Down on the salt flats on the road to the lighthouse,' answered the boy. 'She can't come again. Her father won't bring her. He's away today.'

'And who are *you*?' asked the doctor. 'Her brother? Why can't you bring her?'

'I'm not her brother,' said Mustapha simply, 'I'm nobody; just a street boy. Her father will not let me bring her once he comes back.'

'And her mother?' enquired the doctor. 'Why doesn't she come?'

'She had a new baby this afternoon,' explained Mustapha. 'She is still too weak.'

'Very well,' said the doctor, 'I'll go myself. You must show me the house now. I have to visit a man outside the town and it's not much farther to drive on to the salt fields. Come along!'

Mustapha beamed. He had never before travelled in a private car, and the prospect thrilled him. He was for starting at once, but once more the doctor detained him.

'And you,' he said, 'you look very cold. Haven't you a cloak?'

'This is my cloak,' replied Mustapha. 'It is round the little girl.'

'And is there no blanket to wrap her in?'

'No; the baby born this afternoon was wrapped in the blanket. She has no other.'

'Then I think you had better leave your cloak to keep her warm. I think I can find you something else.'

He ran upstairs two steps at a time and Mustapha waited, quite dazed. Whatever was going to happen next? Surely it couldn't mean that the doctor was going to give him clothes? But he did! Among the Christmas gifts for the hospital was a bale of old clothing. There was a warm coat and pullover just right for Mustapha, and little woolly coats for the fisherman's children. He pulled them out and ran gaily downstairs.

'See,' he said, holding them up. 'These will keep you warm.'

Mustapha stared dumb and unbelieving. He did not understand this sort of thing. Perhaps the doctor was trying to sell them . . . but perhaps he wasn't.

'I have no money,' he whispered uncertainly.

'That's all right,' said the doctor. 'It's a present. We all give presents at our Feast.'

He held the baby, while Mustapha struggled into his new clothes. They were old and darned, but warm, and Mustapha felt like a prince in them. He had never had such garments before. Then, rather clumsily, they managed, between them, to dress the baby, who was screaming again.

'Now come along,' said the doctor, but as he passed the room on the left he popped his head in to say goodbye to the Sunday School party that was about to break up. He came out with a handful of nuts and sweets and biscuits.

'There,' he said, holding them out. 'You shall share our party.'

Mustapha wasn't sure whether life was real any longer or not. He found himself whizzing throught the lighted streets, warm and cosy, and nibbling sugar biscuits. There! They'd passed a bus, and there the policeman was waving his hand to beckon them through – down the bright Boulevard in a stream of cars – getting up speed on the straight lighthouse road. It was heavenly.

They went straight to the fisher's hut, and the doctor was glad he had taken the baby home because the scene there was so like Bethlehem that it made Christmas seem more real. The hut was so poor that it might well have been a stable, with the little donkey asleep now on a heap of straw, and the woman, young, tired and a stranger, with the baby at her breast, immortal symbols of the Love of God.

She was wating anxiously for Mustapha's return, but had not expected him so soon. She looked a little worried as the doctor entered, for she had no money in the house till her husband came home, and he would not be at all pleased if she ran up a bill in his absence. But she smiled when they laid the little girl down beside her, none the worse for her adventures.

'There,' said the doctor, 'she's had her needle and she'll be all right. Keep her warm and give her plenty to drink and I'll be in tomorrow. See, we have put her on a woolly coat, and here's one for her brother.'

'But I have no money,' said the woman nervously.

'That's all right,' said the doctor. He was kneeling on the mud floor, peeping at the tiny, crumpled newcomer blinking at him from between the folds of the blanket. He had forgotten that one usually charged a fee for a visit. No one paid anything at Bethlehem.

Mustapha followed the doctor out into the starlight. They crossed the flats by the light of his torch. It was getting on for 9 p.m., and he wanted a lift back into town.

'Where do you sleep?' asked the doctor as the lamps of the city came into sight round a bend in the road.

The boy hesitated. He had not yet decided where he would sleep. The cafés all seemed pretty dreary after the strange experiences of that evening. He suddenly realized that he had got to go back from this new world that he had entered for a few moments, where men loved and gave and little children laughed and played. Tomorrow he would grab and steal and fight and swear again, and those three different hours would all seem like a dream.

'I don't know,' he said at last, in rather a desolate voice, 'drop me in the market.'

'I know somewhere where you can spend the night,' said the doctor kindly. 'There's a woman near the hospital who keeps a room for boys; no, there's nothing to pay – she does it because she's sorry for them. She'll let you have a blanket.

We'll go along and ask her.'

The doctor's visit took only a few minutes and they were speeding up the hill again. Mustapha had almost come to an end of wondering what would happen next. They stopped in front of a little house in a narrow street near a water pump. By the light of a lamp women and girls were still filling their buckets and they called out friendly greetings to the doctor, who seemed to be well known.

He knocked at the door and it was opened at once by a merry-looking woman with a baby in her arms. At the sound of the doctor's voice the whole family ran to the door and urged him to come in and have supper with them. He entered, and they all sat down again round the bowl of steaming mush and the charcoal pot – father and mother, grown-up daughters, a baby and five scruffy street urchins like himself. He knew them a little, for they all shared the same hunting grounds and they all, like him, were mountain boys driven to the streets by hunger and homelessness. He had often wondered where they dossed down at night, but they had never betrayed their secret, for this was a Christian household and they might get into trouble for going there.

The family itself was a tribal family. They had the brown skin, broad cheekbones, and strong muscles of the mountain-born. Their house was small, poorly furnished but clean, and the boys had a room to themselves on the roof. They were all pleased to see the doctor, and the family smiled welcomingly at Mustapha, but the boys stared suspiciously. They were a gang, and another member meant less room; also on nights when they failed to scrounge for themselves and Zohra took pity on them, it probably meant less supper.

'I've brought you a Christmas present,' said the doctor, his hand on Mustapha's shoulder, 'a new boy.'

'Welcome to him,' replied the women, and they moved up to make room for him at the pot. Mustapha shyly took his place, and one of them broke her piece of bread in two and handed him a scoop. It was the rough food of the very poor, but to Mustapha it tasted delicious.

'And now,' said Zohra triumphantly as the doctor, who was glancing at his watch, rose to go, 'you have come on Christmas Eve, and you must read to us.'

She fetched a book from the shelf, and put it in the doctor's hands and he turned the pages and began to read. The boys already looked half-asleep, warm and satisfied, but the women seemed to be hanging on his words and Mustapha too listened as he'd never listened before. For the doctor read of a young woman great with child, and an outcast baby lying in a manger, and Mustapha thought of the fisherman's cottage. Then he read about shepherds (Mustapha had been a shepherd himself once) and the angels' song.

64

'Unto you is born a Saviour. . . . Glory to God in the highest, on earth peace, goodwill toward men.'

Very simply he spoke on those three words. *A Saviour*, outcast that night, but waiting to be received into every humble, contrite heart. The Saviour that God gave because He loved.

On earth, peace. The peace of the heart that knows forgiveness of sin; the peace of a life committed to that Saviour, the peace of knowing that you need never again feel lonely or afraid.

Goodwill toward men. The Love of God born in the heart that accepted the Saviour; the goodwill that makes Christians count all men their brothers, and open their hearts and homes, and help and serve and give – to see Christ wherever the least of His little ones is hungry or naked or sick.

Mustapha sat cross-legged on the floor, his eyes fixed on the doctor's face. He understood very little, but that little had explained a lot. He knew now why the little sick girl had been accepted and cared for, why he had been clothed and fed, why he had been welcomed in out of the dark and given refuge.

It was all most bewildering; he was beginning to feel drowsy. Zohra was telling the boys to take him upstairs and give him a blanket. The doctor had given him a pat on the head and gone off to help fill his baby's stocking.

And outside the stars shone brightly for Christmas Eve, and all over the world men of every kindred and tribe and nation lifted up their hands to God. Christ was born, to preach the Gospel to the poor, to heal the broken-hearted, to preach deliverance to the captives, to set at liberty them that are bruised.

And one bruised little captive, half-seeking, dimly understanding, turned his face to the light of that coming. But in the dens and evil haunts of the city hundreds more slept and woke as usual, neither knowing nor caring.

The Guest

I. The Visit

The old woman woke with a start. Already arrows of sunlight were piercing the cracks in the walls, so the hens were making a terrible commotion outside. It was broad daylight and Springtime, and she had overslept. This was a pity, because it was Friday, and Friday was the great day of the week for Yacoots, and she had her preparations to make.

She rose as quickly as her rheumatism would allow. There was much to do in the next couple of hours: bread to knead, water to fetch from the spring, fire to kindle, and the room to sweep. But it was impossible to think with the hens making that noise, there must be something the matter with them. She hobbled to the door, and the sweet cold air hit her like a blow, so that she closed her eyes for a moment as the birds rushed out to her squawking. When she opened her eyes and was able to look up, it was too late. A small ragged figure was dodging up the mountain side, in and out of the olive trees on nimble feet, and a glance into the hen house told her that the nesting box was empty.

It was the second time that this had happened and her eyes filled with helpless tears. She did not know who the small thief was, but something must be done about it quickly because her eggs were her living. She could still make the journey down to the market with them, although it exhausted her getting back up the hill. Sometimes she wondered how much longer she could go on alone. She needed help badly, but nobody cared. Her only daughter was married to a prosperous shop keeper, who was thoroughly ashamed of his ragged old mother-in-law, although he gave her a little money now and again.

Muttering with vexation she shouldered her water-pot and set out for the well. The day was warming up now, and she lifted her seamed old face to the sunshine and felt her anger draining away.

It was the time of the first almond-blossom, a pink foam among the silver of the olives and the ash-white boughs of the figs. The stream tossed and sparkled, and in a tuft of grass beside the well the first narcissi were bursting out of their sheaths. She smelt them before she saw them, and it was the very scent of Spring. She had always loved beauty, and although she was old and her eyes were rather dim, it could still lift up her heart and renew her. She forgot the thief and only remembered that in two hours Nadia would arrive and she would hear the words of the Book, which were the words of God.

The bucket was heavy and she was tired when she reached the cabin door, but there was no time to lose. Everything must be ready. She put the kettle on the charcoal and carried it outside to where a small spring wind would fan the glow, while she kneaded the bread and put it to rise. Then she washed her floor, shook out the rush mat, fed the hens and polished her precious brass tray. She would not eat or drink till Nadia came for she could not afford to do so twice. But her joy made her strong and she worked eagerly and swiftly, for Friday's work was no common labour. On other days she was just an old woman toiling through her housework, but on Friday she was a hostess preparing a banquet.

The kettle was boiling, the loaf in the heavy pan turned and done to perfection. The room smelt fragrantly of corn and hot bread. She placed her low round table in the sunshine of the doorway, placed the coffee-pot and glasses on it, then pulled out the box from under her bed and brought out the Book, touching it reverently with fingers that trembled a little. It was a shabby discoloured little book with a faded paper cover, and she had had it for fifteen years. She was not a mountain woman. She had been brought up and married in the town by the Mediterranean Sea, and had borne a little daughter called Anisa.

But her husband had left her when the child was still small, and she had gone to work with a Spanish lady who had been very kind to her. Neither knew the other's language beyond kitchen terms, and they had not been able to communicate much: but the gentleness and kindness had been something not of this world. It seemed to come from God, and its origin was the black book which the Senora read every night with her children at bedtime. Sometimes she tried to tell Yacoots about it, but Yacoots never understood much. She only knew it was a source of love, and when she dusted the room and no-one was looking, she would dare lay her hand on it – just to kiss it.

The Senora's husband had helped Anisa through school, and at fifteen the girl had married a country merchant and gone to live in the mountains. She had borne several sons while Yacoots stayed on in the town, until one day her beloved Senora had broken the news that they were going back to Spain, and Yacoots must find another home.

It had been the greatest sorrow of her rather sad life. The Senora's children were as her children, and when the time came to say goodbye, she was dazed with grief, hardly noticing the glorious gifts that had been given her. Only one thing comforted her. Just before they left her mistress called her apart and put a small paper book into her hand, written not in Spanish, but in Yacoots' own language.

'This part of the book we read every day,' she had explained. 'It tells about Jesus and the way to God. Keep it carefully, and when your grandchildren grow older, ask them to read it to you. It is the word of God.'

They left the same afternoon, and she went to the Port and waved them off with the tears streaming down her face. Then she had gone home, packed her box with the book, wrapped in a handkerchief, at the bottom, and joined her daughter in the mountains.

But the home was small, the boys rough and noisy, and her son-in-law did not want her. It was soon quite clear that there was no room for her, but Senora had left her some money. Between them they had bought the cabin and the patch of land, and there she had lived for fifteen years with her hens and her vegetables, and the only great event in her life had been the birth of Nadia, twelve years previously.

She had never shown her book to anyone until a short time ago, and of course she could not read a word. Her son-in-law was a strict Moslem, and would have called it blasphemy, and Anisa and the boys, although they were fond of her, would have laughed at the idea of an old woman like her wanting to read anything. But on that great day when her grandson came speeding through the olives calling, 'Come, mother's had a girl,' she had known things would be different in the future. And bending over the cradle, looking deep into those wise dark eyes, her heart had told her that one day she and her grand-daughter would read the book together, and then she would hear the voice of God.

She had waited patiently, never hurrying, and the child had loved her from the very beginning. When Nadia was ill or sad, it was Granny she cried for, and her mother, busy with the home and her sons, called grand-mother and was glad to have someone who could give undivided attention to her rather delicate little daughter. Yacoots gave up her hens for those first six years, and became nurse to the little girl. Then Nadia went to school, and she returned home and took up the threads of her old life, but with one difference: on Sundays she always went to her daughter's house, and on Fridays Nadia always came to visit her.

Nadia grew, straight and beautiful, like young trees in Spring, thought her Granny. She brought her school books every week to show off her progress, and at twelve years old she was a fluent reader in two languages. And one day, about four months past, with a beating heart and trembling hands, Yacoots had brought out the book and told the child about the Senora and her gift. 'It is about God and love,' she had said rather vaguely. 'For fifteen years it has been hidden in my box. I have never been able to read it.'

And Nadia, who had no books but her school books and who loved reading, was thrilled. She sat down at once to peruse it laughing at first because it was nothing but a list of names, and then suddenly becoming absorbed in the story. And Yacoots, watching her intently, would never forget that picture. Nadia sat in the doorway in the pale winter sunshine, and the poplars at the well made a background of gold to her grave young face. At last she looked up, dark eyes shining.

'It is a good book, Granny,' she said. 'We will read it together. Every week I will read you a chapter.' Patiently she had stumbled through the genealogy, and then started with relief on the fantastic words of the narrative. And after she had kissed her Granny and gone home, Yacoots had sat for a long time staring out into the sunset and the dusk, repeating the words that had stuck fast in her mind: 'Thou shalt call His name Jesus because He shall save His people from their sins;' and from that day Jesus had become a Person, a Friend who cheered her lonely little cabin. She did not know who He was, nor that He had died and risen again. But something taught her that He was a living present factor, the lodestar of her life. And every Friday He spoke to her again.

II.   The Jewel

'Hello, Granny, it is not yet midday, and you are fast asleep.'

Yacoots jerked herself back to the present and focussed on the figure in the doorway. She had not been asleep, only reliving the past, and for a moment she was surprised that there was no backround of golden poplars – only the shimmer of young green, and a halo of Spring sunshine round Nadia's dark head. The child was laughing and flushed with running, and they greeted each other with that mutual sense of homecoming with which they always started the ritual of Friday.

For it was a sort of ritual – every act leading up to the sacred climax. They started with breakfast. Yacoots could not afford coffee very often and brewed it with extreme care, to drink with the bread, hot from the pan, while Nadia sat cross-legged on the mat and poured out the news of the week. She was a merry vivid child, and it lost nothing in the telling; their neighbourhood had a new baby and Nadia had been considered old enough to go to the Seventh-day feast, and her father had given her a long blue embroidered dress covered in white lace – yes, she would dress up in it on Sunday for Granny's benefit. The baby had worn a little gold cap and had screamed all the time and kept being sick because there were many, many people and the room was so hot. Her brothers were quarrelling because they too wanted new clothes, but their father was saving up to visit the Prophet's tomb in Mecca and said they must wait. The floods had carried away part of the river bank and two goats had been drowned, and their owners were going to sue the town Council. A thief had got in through her cousin's roof-top and stolen her golden bracelets; but at this point Yacoots remembered her own thief and told Nadia about him.

'I wanted to fry you eggs for breakfast,' she said sadly, 'but he took them all. He was small and ragged and barefoot, and he ran very fast.'

Nadia nodded gravely. 'I think that would be Rachid, Granny,' she said. 'His father died and his mother married again and has gone away. His step-father would not have him. He roams the hills and works on farms, but he does not come near the town lest the police should put him in the poor-house. Watch well, Granny. If it is he, we will tell the police and they will beat him.'

Yacoots agreed that this was a sensible thing to do, but Nadia looked out thoughtfully. 'Anyone could steal your eggs, Granny,' she said. 'You need a big fierce dog.'

'But how could I feed it? I can hardly feed myself.'

Nadia could think of no way out of this difficulty. 'I will ask my father,' she murmured, and she sighed. It was her polite way of saying that there was really nothing to be done about the problem and there was a moment of sad silence. It always troubled Nadia that her prosperous father cared so little about her old Granny.

But Yacoots, sensitive as she was to the child's words, hardly noticed, for the great moment of the day was approaching. Nadia cleared the breakfast things, Yacoots swept the crumbs, and they were ready. They drew the curtain across the doorway and settled themselves in a corner of the room. Nadia opened the Book.

'It's chapter 18 today, Granny,' she announced. 'Do you remember what chapter 17 was about?'

It always amused Nadia that her granny loved the Book so much and yet remembered so little of it. But, truth to tell, Yacoots never attempted to take in much. Nadia read in a fast sing-song manner, and most of it flowed over her granny's head. But every week, out of the confusion of words, the old woman gathered one or two jewels of thought or precept, and on these her spirit lived and fed for the rest of the week. She would remember them when she woke, and as she worked in her cabin and little garden strength flowed from them. 'Come unto Me, all who are tired and carry heavy burdens, and I will give you rest,' had been one of her brightest jewels, because of course that meant her and her waterpots. She would murmur the words as she went to the well, and the buckets had never seemed so heavy since. And as she meditated on the words they grew in depth and meaning and seemed to lead to God. But on Friday morning she would lay last week's words away, like jewels discarded, in the storehouse of her memory and wait for a new word. And it was always given. The Book never failed her.

She smiled at the twinkle in Nadia's eye. 'Jesus climbed a mountain, and His clothes and His face shone, and God said, "This is My Son,"' she replied. 'And there was a fish with some money in its mouth.'

'And what else, Granny?'

'I do not remember anything else. That was enough. All this week I have seen that brightness much brighter than the sun at noonday. It has shone in my heart like love. What more should I need to hear?'

Nadia sighed and gave up the examination. Her granny's watery old eyes were fixed on her expectantly. She found the chapter and started to read. What a strange book of contrasts it was, she thought. One week all about the shining glory of God's voice from Heaven, and the next all about little children, lost sheep and quarrelling servants. Strange that a Holy Book should concern itself with such mundane affairs. She wondered what her granny would make of it.

She did not realize that, once having found her jewel, granny usually ceased to register and very seldom heard the end of the chapter at all. And today she found it in verses three and four – words so staggering that having heard them, Yacoots became completely unconscious, not only of the reading, but of Nadia herself. Absorbed in the possible implications of her new jewel, she was only jerked back to reality by a small prod of Nadia's bare foot.

'Granny, didn't you listen? That was a good story about that servant, wasn't it? I think he deserved to go to prison.'

'To go to prison?' Yacoots blinked vaguely. 'Who went to prison, my daughter?'

'Granny!' Nadia was really shocked. 'I read it

so nicely and slowly and I don't believe you heard a word!'

'Indeed, I heard every word!' retorted Yacoots equally shocked. 'It was all about a little child. . . . If you receive a little child, you receive Me. Now what could that mean, my child?'

But Nadia had no idea what it meant, and was only really interested in the stories. She was greatly taken with the parable of the unforgiving servant. It appealed to her sense of humour and justice. She retold it all to her granny, vividly and with actions, and they discussed the rights and wrongs of it and laughed together, until Nadia noticed the long shadows of the poplars and jumped to her feet.

'It's nearly sunset, Granny,' she said. 'I must run.'

She skipped to the well, refilled the bucket, kissed the old woman on both cheeks and made her promise to come on Sunday. Yacoots watched her feet twinkling up the hill, until she was lost to sight in the olives.

And now Yacoots was alone, and this was her hour, the climax of her week. Dearly as she loved Nadia she loved to be alone – alone with the tender colours of the sky, and the voice of her Beloved. She sat perfectly still in the doorway, her hands folded on her lap, staring out into the Spring twilight. She felt she had discovered some tremendous new secret, some key that would open a new door. And yet the secret was a story written in words she could not understand, and the key would not fit the lock.

'Who so receives a little child receives Me . . . Jesus whose name means God with us.' It was the first tangible practical instruction she had ever been given about receiving Him, and yet the meaning evaded her. She knew that He had come by the sense of comfort and protection that surrounded her on winter nights when the storms shook the hut, by the joy she felt in seeking to found her life on His precepts, by the sorrow that engulfed her when she failed and His footsteps eluded her; but this was something much more definite. She could receive a child, and in some new untried way she could receive her Lord.

But what little child? And where was he? There were dozens of children in the farms on the hillside around her, noisy little creatures with spotty heads and running noses, who chased her hens and trampled her garden and with whom she waged perpetual warfare; but surely it could not mean one of these? She grew tired of wondering and it was getting cold. The sky had clouded over, and it smelt of rain and green things growing.

Tonight she would lie down and sleep and trust that the morrow would bring some fresh revelation. She did not know how to pray, but she could look at the stars through a hole in the thatch and hope and wish; and often while she slept understanding was given, and something happened as the week passed to light up her jewels.

But that night there were no stars and the rain

came down in torrents. Yacoots shivered under the ragged blanket and groaned because of her rheumatism, passing the night sleeping and waking. But every time she dozed off, she dreamed of a small heavenly visitor, with eyes like Nadia's creeping in to take refuge from the storm.

III. The Child

Somewhere near the dawn she fell deeply asleep and would have slept right on through the morning had she not been awoken again by a tremendous commotion in the hen-house; but this time it only penetrated her happy dreams slowly and she could not hurry. The wet night had affected her badly and every joint felt set and stiff. The rain had dripped through the hole in the thatch and the raw air made her cough and wheeze. By the time she had wrapped herself in a blanket and hobbled through the mud to the hen-house the birds had settled again, but the nesting box was empty.

Yacoots sat down painfully on the sack of grain and began to cry – weak tears of despair. She just did not know what to do. No doubt, early next morning he would come again. What was there ever to stop him? She could not sit there all night long, and the police would never really bother about an old woman and five eggs.

If only she had a fierce dog, but how could she feed him? Never had she felt more helpless and alone. Yet for her it was the dark hour before the dawn; for almost without realizing it she cried out in the stuffy gloom, 'I can't go on any longer, I need help.'

The sound of her quavering voice startled her. To whom had she spoken? Not to the restless squawking hens, nor yet to her poor shivering self. There was someone else in the hen-house, and she somehow felt that her words had reached an ear that heard and a heart that cared. She did not know anything about prayer, and yet she had prayed. She had made her greatest discovery yet: that the Man who spoke to her in the Book and whose presence comforted her in the wet nights could also hear, and with that thought came a flood of joy. She could tell Him everything for ever, all her fears and helplessness and loneliness. What would happen after that she had not the slightest idea, but even the telling was comfort unspeakable – like the laying down of a burden too heavy to be borne.

She sat quietly for a long time letting the meaning of this discovery unfold itself; and then an idea came into her mind, so insistent that it seemed as though someone had spoken. 'Get up, and go and look for the child who stole the eggs.'

She thought this over for a long time, and the more she thought about it, the more sensible it seemed. What was the use of sitting there waiting to be robbed? Nadia had even said she knew the child who had done it. She would never dare go to the police herself; she had kept clear of them all her life, but surely for Nadia's sake her son-in-law would plead her cause and have the child caught and shut up where he deserved to be. She clenched her fists at the very thought of him. Of course she had never seen him, and could not actually prove who had done it but surely someone would help her.

She fed the hens hastily. Everything else could wait. Later she would mop up the water from the floor and go to the well. Nothing mattered but to follow this urgent instinct and bring this child to justice. Her anger strengthened her, and she needed strength, for the steep path leading up to the main road through the olive groves was a river of liquid mud and the rain was still falling. It would be a miserable expedition with her rheumatism stabbing her at every step, but go she must. She tied her red and white striped cloth round her, threw a sheet-like garment over her head and started the climb.

It seemed at first as though she took one step forward and two backward, and yet when she paused for breath she found she had made headway. Soaked through, she stumbled on, clutching at the olive boughs, leaning against their trunks. She was spattered with mud to her knees when she reached the little platform of land halfway up the hill, too tired to go on. She would crouch under the eaves of the deserted farm hut that stood there and rest for a while. It had been deserted for so long that she did not even know who had lived there. It was a nice ruin, with its mud and dung walls crumbling and its roof mostly fallen in, and in such a wet, draughty position that no one had even wanted to rebuild – a desolate place, thought Yacoots, huddled on its lee side sheltered from the rain, and wondering for the hundredth time why she had ever started on this crazy expedition.

And then she heard the sound that was neither the rustling of leaves nor the patter of rain. It came from inside the shack, and it sounded as though someone was coughing.

She listened intently; something was whimpering and then coughing again. Perhaps it was a sick dog or fox, for no one could live in such a ruin. It was an eerie sound and she gave a little shudder as, weariness forgotten, she started for the path. But even as her foot slithered in the mud she stopped, arrested. The whimpering was louder, and it came from no animal. It was the unmistakable cry of a child in pain, and quite a young child too.

Cautiously, fearfully, she paddled round to the door and peered in, ready to run if she saw anything supernatural. At first she could see nothing at all but dust, gloom, and then, as her eyes grew accustomed, she saw a little figure huddled in some straw, its face hidden in its sleeve. It seemed half asleep and yet coughed and whimpered in turns, and sometimes it shivered. Yacoots watched it for a long time and then decided there was nothing to be afraid of. It was merely a sick little boy . . . a child.

She stepped over the rubble and squatted down on the straw and laid her hand on the ragged jelab.[1] Even through it she could feel the burning temperature of his body. He started violently at her touch and raised himself on his elbow, and when he saw her, he cringed away from her. He was only about nine years old, thin and very dirty, his face flushed and his eyes fever-bright.

'What is the matter, my little boy?' she asked. 'Why do you lie here? Where is your home?'

He relaxed and turned towards her, his head pillowed on his arm. 'I have no home,' he said, 'I look after the sheep and I live here.'

'By yourself?'

He nodded forlornly. After a pause he said, 'Bring me some water.'

She went outside, found a piece of old shard and scooped rain water from a hollow. He drank eagerly and started coughing and shivering again, gazing up at her. She had thrown her own haik[2] round him, and she looked to him like some comforting angel – or like his granny, who had loved him and died. 'Stay with me,' he said, 'don't leave me.'

She stared back, bemused, pondering his

[1] Loose outer garment with hood.
[2] White sheet-like outer garment.

84

words. They had touched some chord, but she could not quite remember what. Now it was coming back; 'Don't leave me . . . receive me . . . a little child, and you'll receive Me.' Perhaps this was the child she was looking for. There was no difficulty at all about how to receive this one. He needed shelter and food and water, and he was filthy. She jerked herself back to practical details, but her heart was beating fast with excitement.

'Have you no parents?' she asked.

He shook his head. 'My father died,' he explained. 'My mother married again. Her husband took her back to the village with their children. He left me with a weaver, but I ran away.'

'Why did you run away?'

'Because he beat me all day long.'

'And now?'

'I work for a shepherd. I look after his sheep and goats. He gives me food and a little money, and I sleep here. But when I tried to go to work today my head felt dizzy, so I went to sleep again.'

'It is cold and wet here,' she said thoughtfully. 'You had better come home with me. I have a blanket and fire and food.'

He made a quick little movement towards her, and as he did so, three eggs rolled out from under his jelab. She suddenly realized that this was the thief she had come to look for; but, strange to say, she was not angry any more. She picked up the eggs, found three others in the straw and tied them into her girdle while he rolled away from her and burst into tears. Of course she would not help him now. It was as though the door of paradise had been opened and then slammed again in his face.

It was all most confusing. Surely the Lord whom she was receiving had nothing to do with stolen eggs, and yet she was quite sure that this must be the child, and her only concern was to get him to her home as quickly as possible. There would be plenty of time to think out these problems in the night when he lay in her bed under her blanket and she shivered beside him.

'Come,' she said, 'I will help you down the path. You know where my hut is.'

He stared at her unbelievingly. He had learned to trust no one, and perhaps this was just a trap to hand him over to the police. Yet she looked neither angry nor cunning, just old and simple and kind, and he wanted to stay with her more than anything else in the world.

'Come,' she said again, holding out her hand. 'It is not raining so hard now. Let us go quickly.'

Perhaps it was all part of those feverish nightmares he had been having; but the old woman was going, and he was going with her. He scrambled to his feet and snuggled under her haik, and together they slithered down the muddy path, she clutching the eggs, and he clutching her, breathless with coughing. By the time they reached the hut he was shivering again and only too ready to collapse on her mattress and pull her blanket over him. After all those lonely, fighting dare-devil months he had come home.

And now she was ready to receive her Lord. She fetched water and all the rest of her charcoal to make a roaring, extravagant glow, and a beautiful warmth pervaded the dark room. She kneaded her bread, recklessly emptied the coffee tin and fried two eggs. Tomorrow could take care of itself. Today she was entertaining a royal guest, and all must be lavish. She sat beside him on the floor and fed him with hot food and drink, and bathed his burning face and hands. She even produced a bottle of cough mixture that the doctor at the hospital had once given her for bronchitis and over-dosed him copiously. He glowed with happiness and warmth, and wonder and fell into a restless sleep.

She stayed beside him all day, and late in the afternoon she was conscious of a strange light in the room and tiptoed outside into the fresh washed air. Over the mountains great purple storm-clouds were massed, but across the valley the sun had broken through low on the horizon, turning the thin rain to silver, and right over her house in a sweeping arch hung a perfect rainbow. She was not in the least surprised. His clothes had shone like the light and his face like the sun, so why not a rainbow to encircle the sleeping child? She went in again and baked some more bread and boiled up some barley soup. Then the rain stopped, the storm clouds rolled towards the sea and the stars came out.

There was no other blanket in the house and nowhere to lie except on the floor, so sleep was difficult, but Yacoots did not want to sleep. She crouched by the dying charcoal fire, sometimes dozing a little but mostly absorbed in the wonder of what had happened. It mattered to her no longer that the child was a thief and an outlaw. A child's hands are the same all the world over, and his hands had clung to her and his eyes had besought her. 'Stay with me,' he had said. 'Don't leave me,' and she found her own heart echoing the words, 'Stay with me, don't leave me,' and she wondered again, 'To whom am I speaking? To the child or to the One in whose name I received the child?' But this was too much for her poor old brain, and she gave up.

The room was bright with moonlight, and she turned to look at the boy; but as she did so she realized something had happened. The perspiration was pouring down his face and his skin was cold. He woke, confused, with his teeth chattering and clung to her again while she rubbed him dry with an old piece of towelling and blew up the fire. Then, she heated up the rest of the coffee and he drank it, leaning up against her in the dark. He kissed her hand and closed his eyes, and she stayed looking down at him for a time and knew that the fever had left him. At last he was sleeping deeply and peacefully.

And that peace seemed to fill the room, emanating from the child who had come home. She had never felt anything like it before. All her wondering, fears and anxieties fell away in the presence of it, and she knew she could just lean back and rest. The night was paling outside, and the cocks were crowing, but the floor no longer seemed hard nor the dawn cold. That peace was like a soft pillow, and she closed her eyes and slept as deeply as the child. On through the bright daybreak, the squawking of the hens and the stir of the morning she slept; and when at last she woke it was to the clatter of buckets, and the child stood in the doorway against the brightness of the noonday sun. His face was pale and peaked and he still coughed. His eyes besought her. He saw that she was awake and he stood watching her anxiously. He had worked so hard. Surely she would notice. Surely she would notice. Surely she could not refuse him!

She looked round, dazzled at first and then with growing astonishment, for her prayers had been answered and help had come. The room was swept and the fire burning, and fresh firewood was stacked round it to dry. Buckets of water stood in a neat row, and the hens, being quiet, had presumably been fed. The child, eager and hungry, stood looking first at her and then at his handiwork. He presented her with a basin of brown eggs.

'I will do it every morning,' he pleaded, 'before I go to the goats. I will bring you fire-wood every day from the mountain, and in the

evening I will dig your garden and grow vegetables. I will fetch you water and sweep your
house, I will. . . .' Imagination failed him and he
flung out his arms to indicate the immensity
of his labours. Then he pulled forward the little
table and sat down expectantly, laughter bub-
bling up in him because he felt sure he had made
his point. With the extreme resilience of the
uncared-for, he seemed to have recovered from
his illness. A cocky little boy, but he did know
how to work!

'There is bread left from yesterday,' he reminded her, 'and see, I have brought you some
goat's cheese. I told the shepherd I was ill, but
when we have eaten I must go back to him . . .
until the evening?'

His voice ended on a question-mark, and
she realized that he was asking to stay, and this
surprised her because she had taken it for
granted that he wanted to stay. Surely the Heavenly guest had come to stay. She had been cutt-
ing the bread, but she glanced up suddenly,
almost expecting to see the shining robes and the
face like light. But all she saw was a little boy
in a filthy jelab sitting grinning cross-legged on
her floor.